The  *nds*

*For Mrs Tai Lihua and her parents
whose lives inspired this story – Y.J.*

*For every child whose life shines
with colours and emotions – Y.R.*

THE VISIBLE SOUNDS is a uclanpublishing book

First published in China in 2021 by
Beijing Dandelion Children's Book House Co. Ltd

This edition published in Great Britain in 2021 by uclanpublishing
University of Central Lancashire, Preston, PR1 2HE, UK

Text copyright © Yin Jianling, 2021
Illustration copyright © Yu Rong, 2021
Translation copyright © Filip Selucky, 2021

978-1-912979-79-0

1 3 5 7 9 10 8 6 4 2

The right of Yin Jianling and Yu Rong and Filip Selucky to be identified
as the author and illustrator and translator of this work respectively
has been asserted in accordance with the Copyright, Designs
and Patents Act 1988.

A CIP catalogue record for this book is available from the British Library.

Printed and bound in Great Britain by Page Bros Ltd,
Mile Cross Lane, Norwich NR6 6SA.

The Visible Sounds

Yin Jianling & Yu Rong

Translated by Filip Selucky

uclanpublishing

When MiLi was two years old,
an illness came into her life.

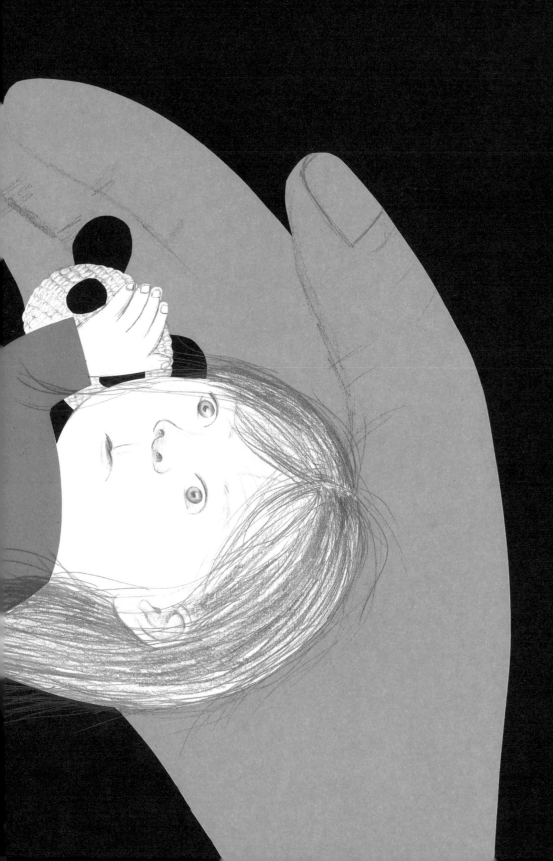

It took all *sounds* away.
They vanished from her world.

MiLi suddenly felt anxious
and upset. Her world was **silent**.

She couldn't express her feelings
in any other way than tears.

MiLi's dad took her to many hospitals.
They couldn't find a doctor who was able to cure her ears.

The old engine made the bus **shake** as if there
was a mischievous tiger hidden inside.

MiLi couldn't help **touching** it with her hand. As she did,
she felt soft **trembling**, as if the small tiger was tickling her palms.
MiLi realised that this was a *sound* and began to laugh!

There was a small
popcorn stand on
the street.

POP

POP

POP

went the corn inside the machine.

Everyone standing around covered their ears.
MiLi didn't need to do that.

When she felt the slight **vibrations** coming
from the ground up to her feet, MiLi knew
that this was a *sound*.

There was a very old
lorry outside the window.
As it was struggling to drive up
the hill, dark clouds of smoke
were **puffing** from its tailpipe.

MiLi knew that
this was also a *sound*.

This is how **sound** returned to MiLi's world.

She could **touch** a **sound** with her hands, she could **see** it with her eyes.

She could **feel** it with her feet and even with her heart.

Sound is a warm wind,
   gently brushing against cheeks
   and softening one's heart.

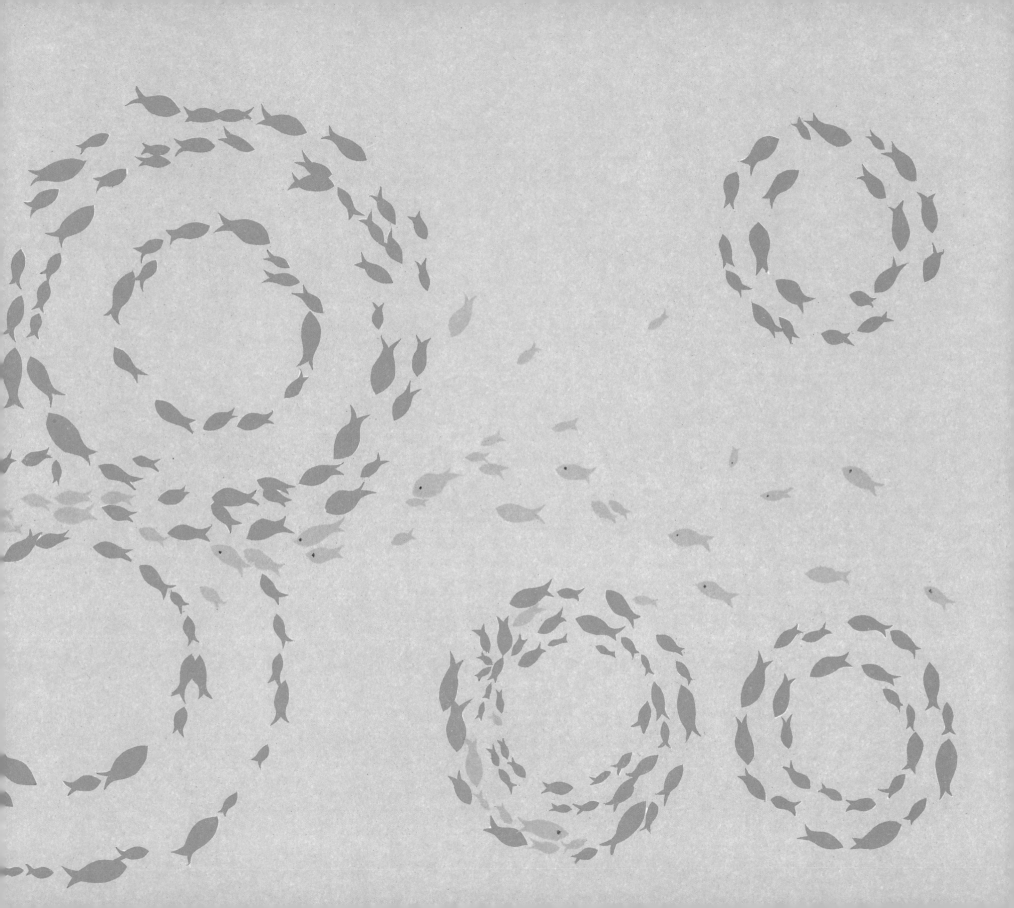

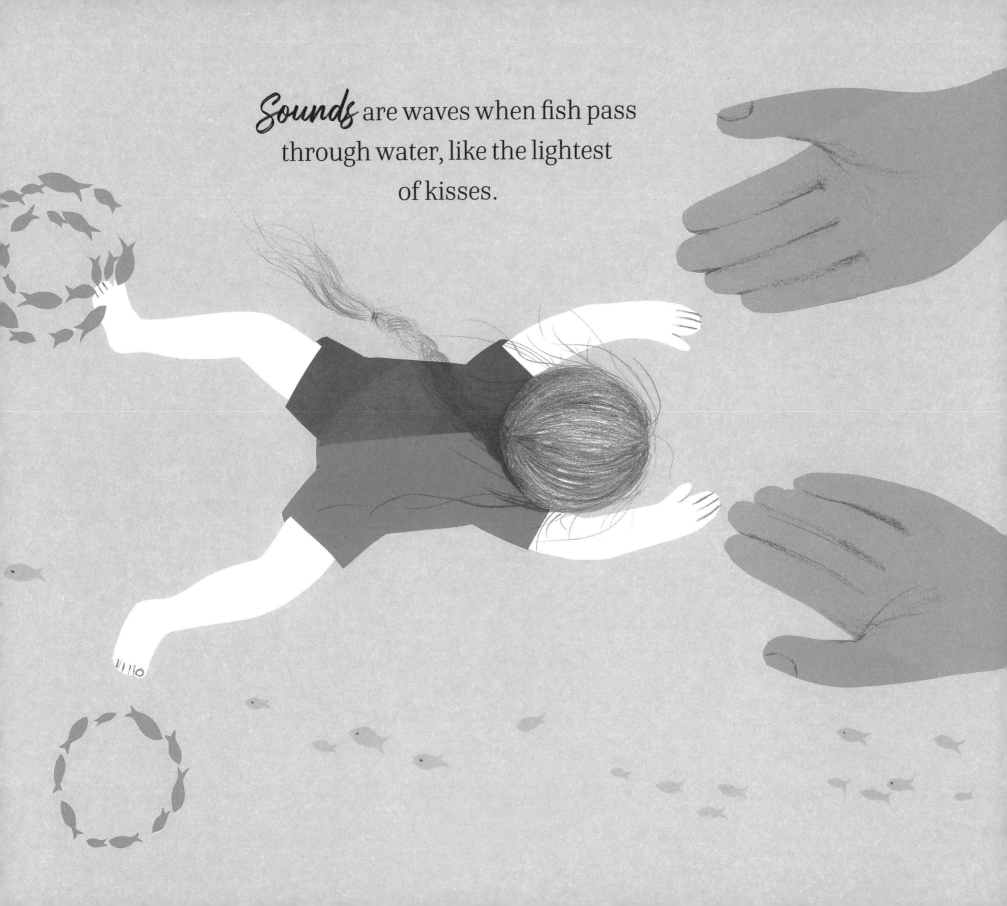

Sounds are waves when fish pass through water, like the lightest of kisses.

Sound changes with the seasons, from emerald green into shiny shades of gold.

Sound is the bright sunshine
flowing into one's blood,
beaming with rays.

People's lips constantly move and change shapes, they are like blooming flowers.

Language is a river, flowing and flooding into MiLi's body.

The river turns into musical notes, like little tadpoles swimming into MiLi's heart . . .

MiLi sings songs with her heart.
The beautiful music **jiggles** in her blood.

It doesn't have a *sound*, but it
shines with colours and emotions . . .

The wooden floor **vibrates** under drumbeats.
MiLi follows the rhythm and
starts dancing to it . . .

To dance without music
is to dance with one's heart.

MiLi's heartbeat **pulses** through
her blood like wind, rain and sunshine.

A body is just like a violin - the heart is the strings,
the breath is the bow. The music coming from one's soul
covers the fields with a velvet greet carpet that **shakes** the sky,
bringing sparkling raindrops to settle on the ground . . .

Although MiLi cannot **hear** anything and her world remains **silent**, it has become vibrant, shining with the *colour* of *sound*.

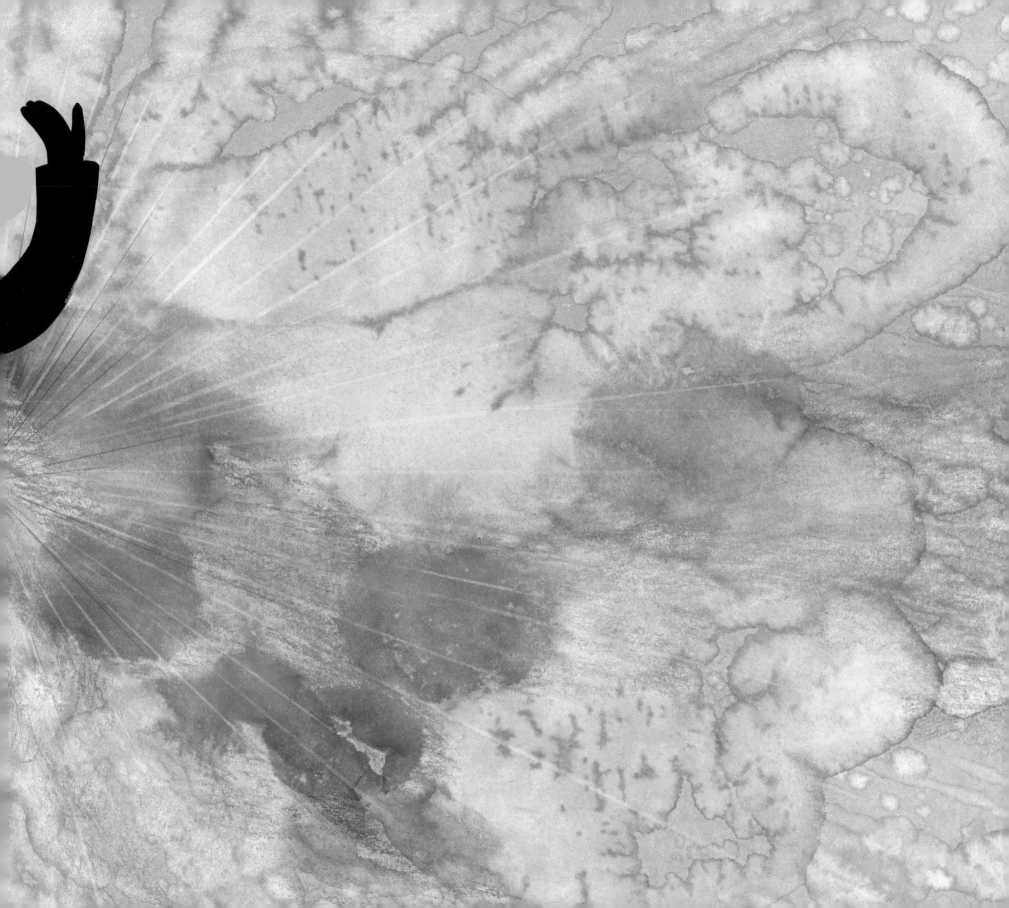

Sign Language

Sign language is not a universal language. It varies across the world, and can even vary in different areas of the same country. This book aims to show the universal love and respect to people who use sign language worldwide. There are three different sign languages used inside:

Chinese Sign Language finger spelling of the Chinese phonetic letter H

Chinese Sign Language finger spelling of the Chinese phonetic letter C

Chinese Sign Language finger spelling of the Chinese phonetic letter I

Chinese Sign Language finger spelling of the Chinese phonetic letter F

Chinese Sign Language finger spelling of the Chinese phonetic letter E

British Sign Language finger spelling of the letter P

British Sign Language finger spelling of the letter C

British Sign Language finger spelling of the letter S

American Sign Language finger spelling of "I love you" (informal)

American Sign Language finger spelling of the number 7

Tai Lihua

This book is inspired by the story of Tai Lihua who was born in 1976 in Yichang City in the Hubei Province of China. When she was two Tai had a fever and shortly after began losing her hearing. When a teacher brought a drum into class and began beating it, Tai was excited to find she could feel its rhythms passing through the whole of her body. Tai started imagining herself dancing to the vibrations she felt from music.

Tai began dancing and despite her teachers sometimes worrying she appeared a little clumsy, Tai never gave up! This determination earned her a place on the world stage as one of the most beautiful and graceful dancers. Tai has performed at the Carnegie Hall in New York and at La Scala in Milan. Her favourite dance is *The Spirit of the Peacock*. People across the globe have been inspired by Tai's dancing and her incredible story.

The name MiLi means grain of rice. In the original Chinese version of the story, the main character was called Tiny Rice so MiLi was chosen to reflect this. In China rice carries association with strength, persistence and having life spirit which fit MiLi's character well.